Feelings

A to Z

Written and Illustrated by

Kathleen Lehigh James

Feelings, A To Z

Copyright © 2002
by
Kathleen Lehigh James

Library of Congress Control Number: 2002103064
International Standard Book Number: 1-930353-51-0

Printed 2002 by
Masthof Press
219 Mill Road
Morgantown, PA 19543-9516

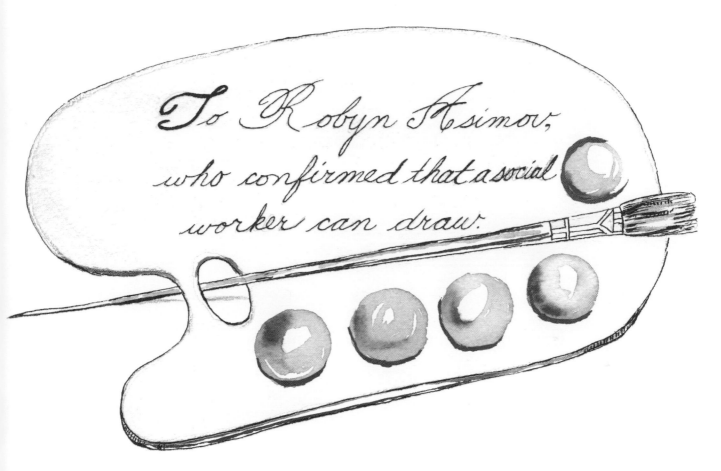

To Robyn Asimov,
who confirmed that a social
worker can draw.

and to my parents
David and Florence Lehigh,
who opened doors for me.

BENCHY

Benchy, a Pennsylvania Dutch nickname for Benjamin, is the son of the author. We follow him in *Feelings A to Z* for a travelogue through the imaginative world of emotions of an eight-year-old boy.

The author is a Licensed Clinical Social Worker at East Orange General Hospital's Outpatient Behavioral Health Program in East Orange, New Jersey. Kathleen is a graduate of Eastern Mennonite University, Harrisonburg, Virginia, and Ohio State University School of Social Work.

Feelings

Feelings are the basic building blocks of your character.

Learning to recognize and to express feelings is an important part of early growth.

If you can name and understand your feelings, then you can choose the ones that make you feel good and happy.

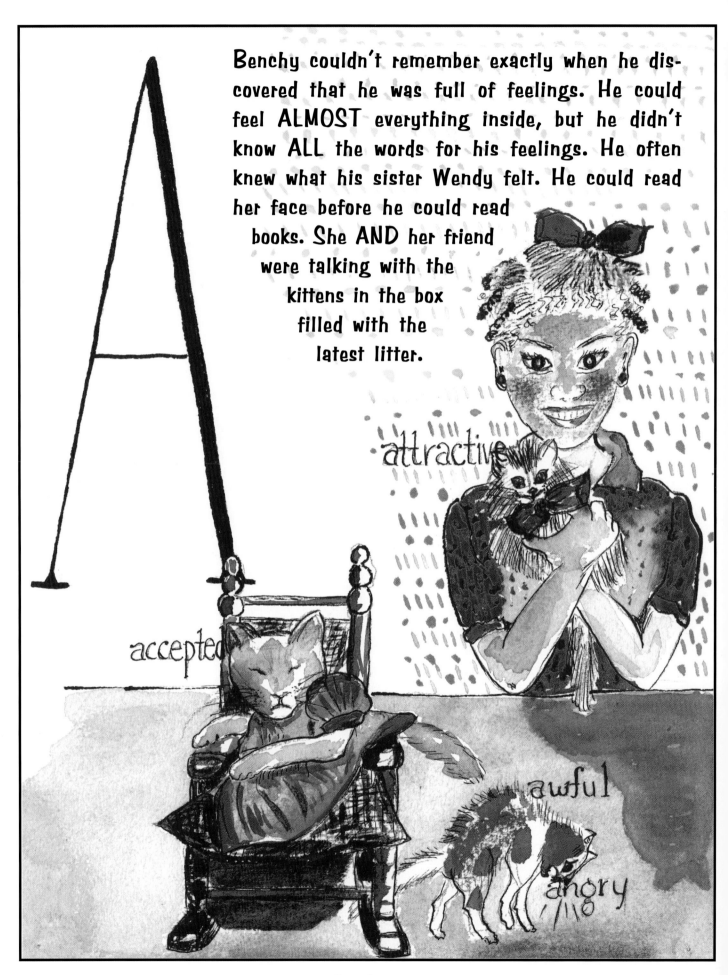

Benchy couldn't remember exactly when he discovered that he was full of feelings. He could feel ALMOST everything inside, but he didn't know ALL the words for his feelings. He often knew what his sister Wendy felt. He could read her face before he could read books. She AND her friend were talking with the kittens in the box filled with the latest litter.

attractive

accepted

awful

angry

Every day, Benchy felt hundreds of different emotions inside. When he stared into Mother Cat's eyes or scrunched on his tummy near a pigeon, the magic happened. When he studied each kitten, he felt his feelings change from one thing to ANOTHER. He felt big grown-up words such as AFFECTION and excitement. And he felt ANGRY that Mom said that they must give AWAY ALL the kittens.

appreciated

affectionate

abandoned
addled

FREE KITTENS

His feelings soared when a BUTTERFLY BRIEFLY perched on his nose for a still second. He gazed cross-eyed at its wobbling antennae and felt BEAUTIFUL.

How did this happen? He couldn't see his feelings. He couldn't touch them, but WOW. They were there—**sure and strong!**

blissful

better

bad
baffled
bewildered

C

Benchy once pulled together a CAPABLE
panel on the beach and asked them:
"How are feelings made?
Is there a motor inside?"

BOARD MEETING
10 ¢ per question
ANSWER QUARANTEED
on all issues
or
MONEY BACK
SPONSORED BY MUM MOM'S, INC.

capable

chagrined

calm

confused

confident

Are feelings whipped up
like egg whites
by a DANDY egg beater?

Are they a trick,
like laying
EGGS?

efficient

Are **FEELINGS** wind-up tunes,
like inside a music box?
Are they **FAIR?**

G

genuine

great

Benchy
wanted to
know who
put GOOD
feelings
inside
him?

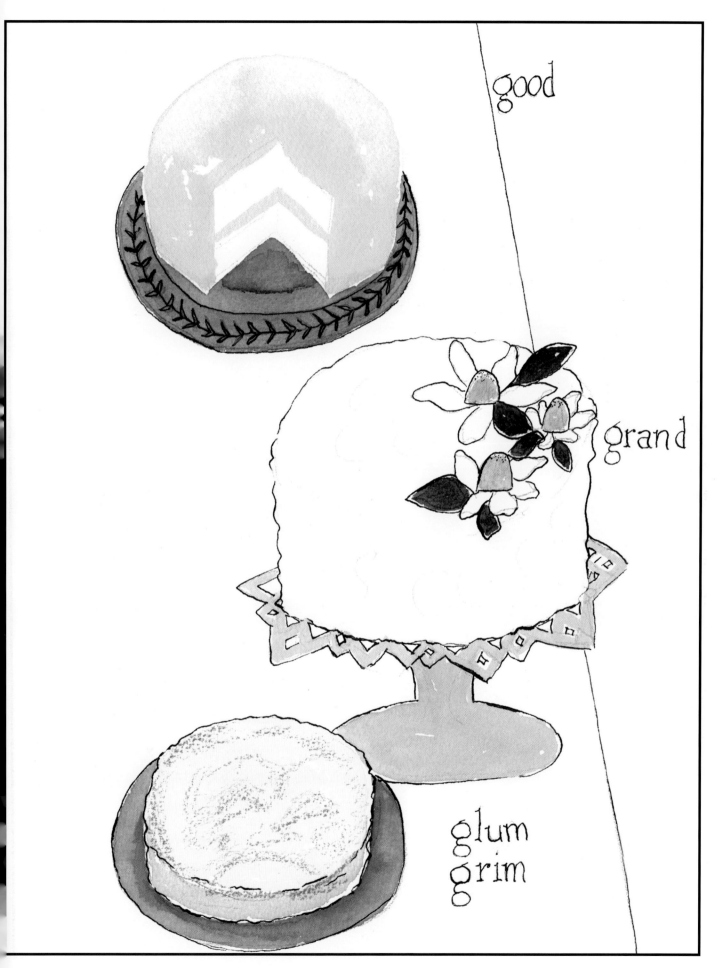

good

grand

glum
grim

happy

helpful

What made him
feel HAPPY, or . . .

hopeful

handy

homesick

hurt

harried

I irked

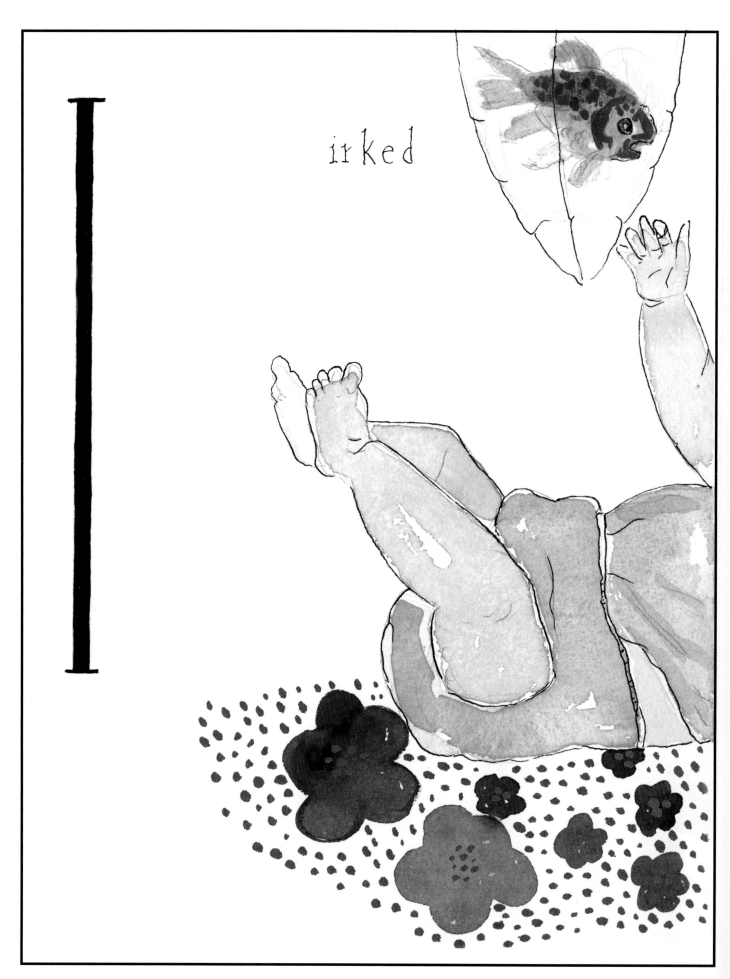

Kaput

What made him KIND?

lacking

lonely

M

mellow

melancholy

Why did Benchy feel MELAN-
CHOLY when his gerbil escaped
and never came back? Was it
his heart?

marvelous

mean

Once, when he had an earache, he felt it pound, "Ka-boom, ka-boom, ka-boom!" Did his heart make feelings?

He made a promise to find the answer NEXT day, to search from Australia to Zanzabar. It felt NICE to look and learn.

neat

nurturing
nice

nasty

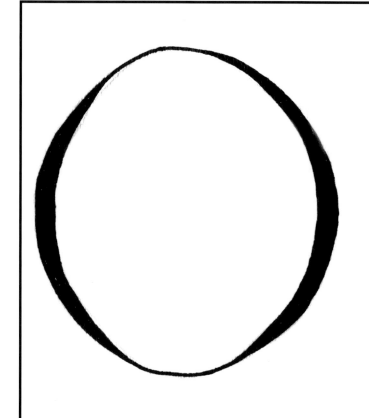

offensive

ostracized

He felt OKAY.

open
okay

positive
pleased
peaceful
productive

He felt PRODUCTIVE.

perplexed

perturbed

pathetic

qualified

He felt
QUALIFIED.

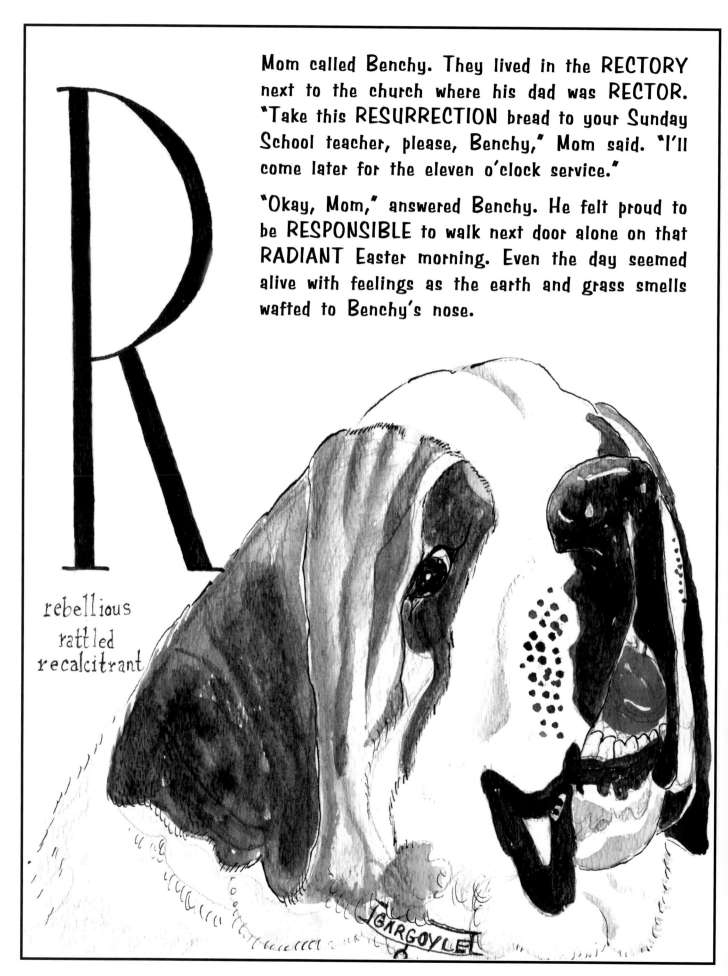

R

rebellious
rattled
recalcitrant

Mom called Benchy. They lived in the RECTORY next to the church where his dad was RECTOR. "Take this RESURRECTION bread to your Sunday School teacher, please, Benchy," Mom said. "I'll come later for the eleven o'clock service."

"Okay, Mom," answered Benchy. He felt proud to be RESPONSIBLE to walk next door alone on that RADIANT Easter morning. Even the day seemed alive with feelings as the earth and grass smells wafted to Benchy's nose.

radiant

relaxed

S

Benchy felt SUPER!

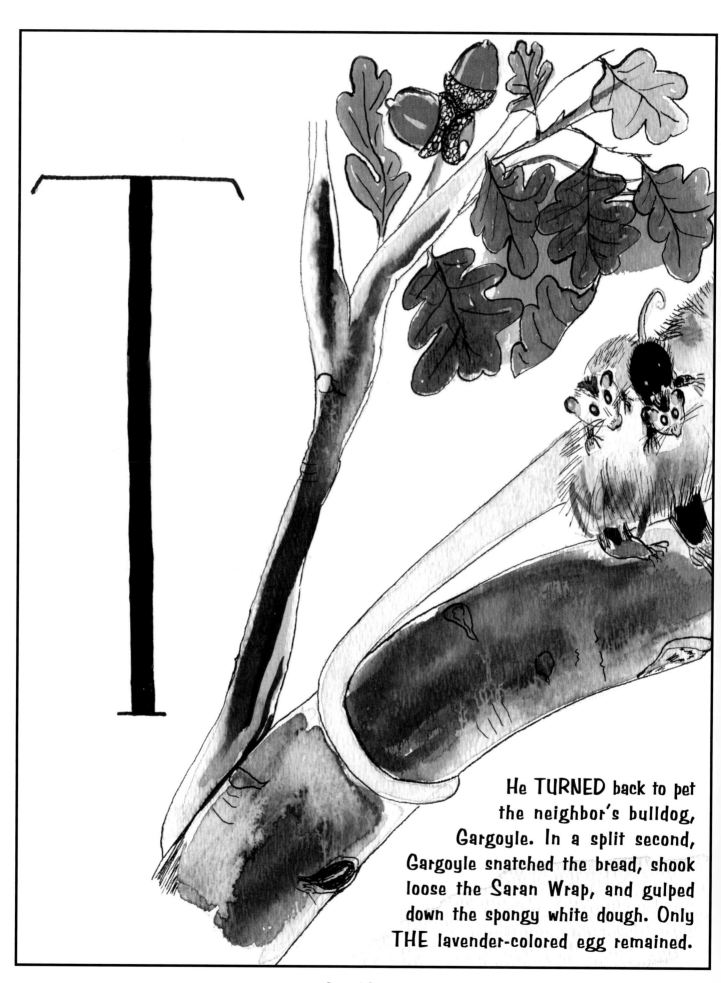

He TURNED back to pet
the neighbor's bulldog,
Gargoyle. In a split second,
Gargoyle snatched the bread, shook
loose the Saran Wrap, and gulped
down the spongy white dough. Only
THE lavender-colored egg remained.

timid

tender

trustworthy

truthful

terrible

terrified

Gargoyle snatched it in his TEETH like a prize and lay down with it in his secret crevice near THE steps. He licked it slowly and glared up TO guard it from Benchy.

unique

unified

ugly
useless

Time stood still. Suddenly, Benchy felt full of fear. What would his teacher and Mom do? How could he go to class empty-handed?

He started to pray. Mom said it was a way to get UGLY feelings out. "Tell God what you're feeling." As he prayed, he felt some answers.

His heart felt lighter; he trusted God.

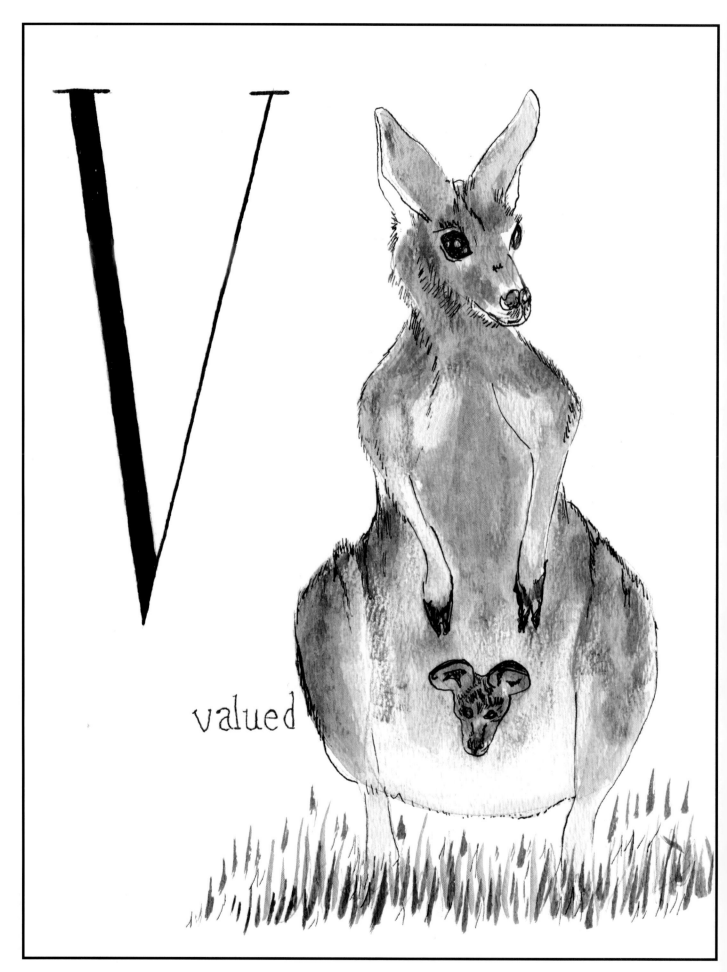

V

valued

He walked slowly towards his Sunday School class that he hoped would be VACANT.

He passed the nursery.
"Happy Easter, Benchy," called Mrs. Small, relaxing with a sleeping baby.

vague

vacant

W

well
whole
worthwhile

Nothing came out of his mouth.
Benchy felt WOEBEGONE and scared.
WHAT WOULD he
tell his teacher?

wasted
woebegone

X

Benchy felt wooden (XYLOID).

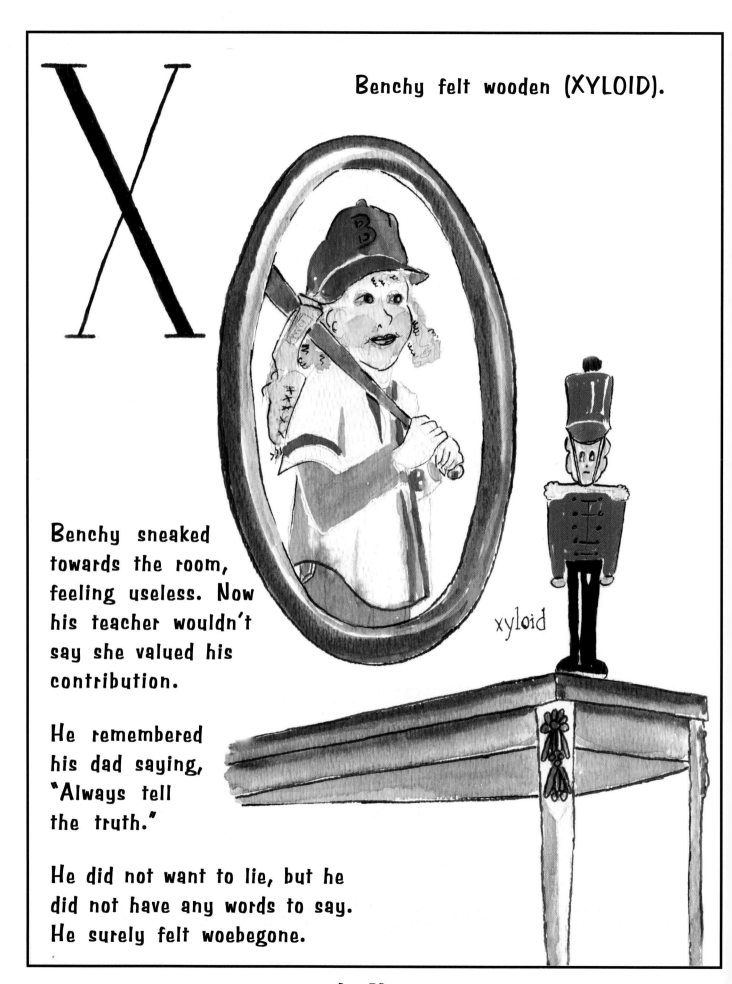

xyloid

Benchy sneaked towards the room, feeling useless. Now his teacher wouldn't say she valued his contribution.

He remembered his dad saying, "Always tell the truth."

He did not want to lie, but he did not have any words to say. He surely felt woebegone.

He imagined asking his great-granddad what to do. Great-granddad was always thinking of heaven (XENOCENTRIC). He would know what was right.

xenocentric

Benchy wanted to run.
How did he get into these
YUCKY dilemmas?

youthful

yukky

Z zealous

He prayed to be ZAPPED with a solution. "Get it out. Say what you feel. Be open. Be honest," went through his mind. Since Benchy was early, his teacher was there alone.

He gulped, "I feel awful. Mom sent you some bread, but I dilly-dallied and Gargoyle ate it. Please forgive me."

She smiled. "You've given me your best gift, Benchy," she said happily as she hugged him.

"You told me your feelings. Yes, I will forgive you."

zestful

zany

zapped

Benchy released his breath,
like a deflating balloon.
It was a miracle. He felt fine again.

"Will you help me tell
my mom?" he asked.

"Of course," laughed his teacher.
"Won't she be surprised she baked
for Gargoyle?"

Benchy laughed, too, feeling sure his mom would understand.

List Other Feelings Here

Make your own Happiness by feeling Loving

Joyful

Peaceful

Helpful

Etc.